Natalie's First Christmas Adventure

NATALIE NOCERA SARABELLA

Archway Publishing books may be ordered through booksellers or by contacting:

Archway Publishing
1663 Liberty Drive
Bloomington, IN 47403
www.archwaypublishing.com
844-669-3957

Scriptures taken from the New King James Version of the Bible.

Philippians 4:12-13
[12] I know what it is to be in need, and I know what it is to have plenty. I have learned the secret of being content in any and every situation, whether well fed or hungry, whether living in plenty or in want. [13] I can do all this through him who gives me strength.

ISBN: 978-1-6657-1409-9 (sc)
ISBN: 978-1-6657-1411-2 (hc)
ISBN: 978-1-6657-1410-5 (e)

Print information available on the last page.

Archway Publishing rev. date: 10/27/2021

Natalie's First Christmas Adventure

FORWARD by Carol Levitt

I have known Natalie since we were 18 yrs old. Her gifts and talents are many and now she opens up her world to children's written storytelling. Natalie is the ultimate artist to take you on a journey both through her paintings and stunning ornaments. Natalie's stories come to life through the eyes of the little girl who always had a dream. This book brings life back to a time when Christmas was truly Magical and expresses how a child's imagination could soar and become a reality. When Natalie enters your world it just "Sparkles."

Acknowledgments

First, I would like to thank my daughter-in-law Raquel for inspiring me to write a children's Christmas book.

My two grandchildren Penelope and Jerry, who enjoy our story time.

A special thanks to my daughter Carrie for running my business remotely while successfully building her own business Snaks 5th Avenchew, a horse and dog gourmet treat company.

To my mom, whom I miss every single day. I carry your love in my heart and you will always be my shotgun girl, I love you Curly.

Additionally, I want to thank my faithful fans and collectors who keep me motivated. I do this for you.

My very special Carol Levitt.

And a very special thank you to Elsan Dzudza, CEO at Visible Motion, who has been my ultimate web guru for many years.

My team at Simon and Schuster/Archway Publishing

Natalie and Carolyn were excited when they woke up on Saturday morning. They have been waiting for this day, and it was finally here. Today was the day they were going to see Santa.

This year's visit was very important for Natalie. She was looking forward to seeing Santa and telling him about the special present she was hoping for this year. Natalie was most excited to get to A&S department store downtown. Her favorite part was the giant Christmas tree that hung from the ceiling in the elevator bank.

This tree was special; her mom would take them every year to see the sparkling tree. The tree was filled with huge ornaments, angels, peppermint candy canes, and millions of jewels and strings of shiny beads. Natalie loved sparkly things!

While waiting for the elevator, Natalie and Carolyn gazed at the tree. Natalie was mesmerized staring at the tree; she imagined herself dancing among the branches of the beautiful baubles. She didn't even hear her sister chattering and pulling her to the waiting elevator.

The elevator doors opened, and in they marched. They got off the elevator on the eighth floor, which was a toy land, complete with a merry-go-round, which was Carolyn's favorite.

But, before they could even get there, the elevator doors closed behind them, and Carolyn's blanky got stuck. She pulled and tugged, but it wouldn't come loose. Then her big sister put her hands around her waist and helped as well. It came loose, and the two of them tumbled backward into the toy department, which made quite the entrance!

After a ride on the merry-go-round, everyone received a ticket to see Santa. When it was Natalie's turn, she just couldn't wait to tell Santa the news.

Natalie climbed up and greeted Santa with a big smile. "Hi, Santa!"

"Well, hello there, Natalie. I know you've been a very good girl; what would you like for Christmas?" asked Santa.

Although Natalie's Christmas list was small, she made sure the most important gift, an artist's easel, was at the top of the list.

She wanted to paint a beautiful Christmas ornament like the ones on her favorite spinning tree; she wanted to enjoy Christmas all year long.

Christmas morning came, and the two sisters ran out of their rooms, heading for the living room. Natalie could see an easel with a huge red bow on top. But before she took the next step, her feet got tangled up in her little sissy's blanky, and she tumbled head over heels, almost crashing into the tree. The blanky had been at the center of another minor catastrophe.

Natalie's stocking was filled with paint, brushes, beads, glitter, and everything she would need to work on her ornament painting.

Not long after breakfast, she started drawing a very large circle right in the center of the canvas. Then she went straight to work!

It didn't take her very long to finish painting her masterpiece. It just needed to dry, and then the fun would begin.

Later that day, Natalie set up the kitchen table with all the Christmas stocking contents. She set up a spot for her little sister too. They worked on the painting, making it more beautiful with every crystal they added.

Finally, it seemed to be done, but Natalie felt there was something missing. What could it be? She thought back to her favorite tree and suddenly remembered. "We need a bow on the top of our ornament painting!"

Natalie looked over to Carolyn, grabbed one of the ribbons from her pigtails, and placed it at the top of the painting. That made it complete. She looked at the painting with pride.

In the months leading up to Christmas, their school was planning a Christmas fair. There was a special prize this year for the best Christmas entry. Natalie knew right away that she was going to paint a great big ornament, just like the one in the department store and on her canvas.

She ran home from school with the flyer in her hand; she couldn't wait to tell Mom. Mom's job was buying the ornaments, and of course she bought the biggest she could find. Carolyn was excited too, so she became the little elf helper.

The next day after school, the girls hurried home and found that Mom had everything set up for them. They were ready to start.

Glitter and glue flew through the air. Natalie said, "This must be what Santa's workshop looks like!"

When the sisters finally finished their beautiful creation, they propped their masterpiece on a shelf to dry and counted the days until the fair would begin.

Natalie and Carolyn waited while the judges walked from desk to desk, visiting every contestant. It looked like a winter wonderland. Everyone had worked very hard on their entries, and they were all beautiful.

Natalie wasn't worried or nervous; she looked down at Carolyn and gave her a little wink. Carolyn gave her big sister's hand a squeeze of encouragement and smiled.

Suddenly, there was the announcement. "And the winner of the grand prize is … Natalie Sarabella and her ultimate ornament."

The girls were so happy they jumped up and down in excitement. They were so pleased and proud to be chosen that they had even forgotten there was a prize.

The prize was for the winners to visit Santa at the North Pole and work with the elves to create a special ornament for Santa to leave on every Christmas tree.

The girls taught the elves how to make the beautiful baubles that won the prize.

Everyone was happy and singing Christmas songs. They helped pack Santa's sleigh, and then out came Santa and Mrs. Claus.

"Let's hurry, everyone! We have to get these girls back," said Mrs. Claus.

And as the last gift was loaded onto the sleigh, Santa said, "Hop in, girls; it's off to Red Hook, Brooklyn, we go!"

All their new friends gave them big waves of goodbye, and then Natalie and Carolyn buckled themselves in. Santa started calling out the reindeer's names, and the sleigh took to the sky.

Natalie and Carolyn knew that this was the best Christmas adventure ever, and they couldn't wait to see where their next journey would take them.

"Follow Your Dreams"